This book is dedicated to anyone who has ever
owned a smelly, stained, muddy, sticky, painty,
VERY loved blanket ♥
— A. M.

To Erin, for endless support and helping me
to remember to eat at deadlines
— K. A.

tiger tales
5 River Road, Suite 128, Wilton, CT 06897
Published in the United States 2017
Originally published in Great Britain 2017
by Little Tiger Press
Text copyright © 2017 Angie Morgan
Illustrations copyright © 2017 Kate Alizadeh
ISBN-13: 978-1-68010-074-7
ISBN-10: 1-68010-074-2
Printed in China
LTP/1400/1805/0217

For more insight and activities,
visit us at www.tigertalesbooks.com

That's MY Blanket, Baby!

by
Angie Morgan • Illustrated by
Kate Alizadeh

tiger tales

Once upon a while ago, there was a brand-new baby named Bella,

who had a brand-new blanket
named Blanket.

Bella **loved** Blanket.
Everywhere Bella went,
Blanket **HAD** to come, too.

Together Bella and Blanket explored the world, and as Bella grew bigger and **bigger . . .**

she grew to love Blanket more and **MORE.**

Bella and Blanket did
everything
together—
like painting stuff,

and sticking
things to other
things,

and singing and dancing in mud puddles.

SPLASH!

Then one day, a brand-new baby arrived who had a brand-new blanket of his own.

Bella **loved** New Baby.
In fact, she loved him almost as much
as she loved Blanket.

But she thought she would love him
even more if . . .

. . . he didn't **cry** as much.
"Don't cry, Baby," said Bella.
But New Baby kept on crying.

So Bella tried
tickling him,

and New Baby
cried —
even
more.

So Bella told him her funniest joke,

but New Baby didn't laugh **at all.**

So Bella showed him her favorite **happy** dance . . .

. . . and New Baby stopped crying.

"But—that's MY blanket, Baby!" cried Bella. "You have a nice NEW blanket of your own."

But New Baby didn't want his boring new blanket.
He wanted Bella's sparkly, muddy, painty, smelly one.

"Oh, dear," said Bella.
She wasn't sure what to do.

So she thought a bit and wondered if,

once upon a while ago, Blanket had
been all clean and new, too.

So she said, "I know, Baby . . . .

"If you take your clean NEW blanket . . ."

everywhere you go . . .

"I will show you how to do stuff like painting, and sticking things to other things,

and singing
and dancing in
mud puddles.

"And when you have grown
as big as me, Baby,
you will love your blanket
ALMOST as much . . .

"as I love you."